Dear Parents:

Congratulations! Your child is taking the first steps on an exciting journey. The destination? Independent reading!

STEP INTO READING® will help your child get there. The program offers five steps to reading success. Each step includes fun stories and colorful art or photographs. In addition to original fiction and books with favorite characters, there are Step into Reading Non-Fiction Readers, Phonics Readers and Boxed Sets, Sticker Readers, and Comic Readers—a complete literacy program with something to interest every child.

Learning to Read, Step by Step!

Ready to Read **Preschool–Kindergarten**
• big type and easy words • rhyme and rhythm • picture clues
For children who know the alphabet and are eager to begin reading.

Reading with Help **Preschool–Grade 1**
• basic vocabulary • short sentences • simple stories
For children who recognize familiar words and sound out new words with help.

Reading on Your Own **Grades 1–3**
• engaging characters • easy-to-follow plots • popular topics
For children who are ready to read on their own.

Reading Paragraphs **Grades 2–3**
• challenging vocabulary • short paragraphs • exciting stories
For newly independent readers who read simple sentences with confidence.

Ready for Chapters **Grades 2–4**
• chapters • longer paragraphs • full-color art
For children who want to take the plunge into chapter books but still like colorful pictures.

STEP INTO READING® is designed to give every child a successful reading experience. The grade levels are only guides; children will progress through the steps at their own speed, developing confidence in their reading.

Remember, a lifetime love of reading starts with a single step!

Text copyright © 2021 by Amy Krouse Rosenthal Revocable Trust
Cover art and interior illustrations copyright © 2021 by Brigette Barrager
Written by Candice Ransom
Illustrations by Lissy Marlin

Visit us on the Web!
StepIntoReading.com
rhcbooks.com

Educators and librarians, for a variety of teaching tools, visit us at RHTeachersLibrarians.com

Library of Congress Cataloging-in-Publication Data
Names: Ransom, Candice F., author. | Barrager, Brigette, illustrator. | Rosenthal, Amy Krouse.
Title: Uni brings spring : an Amy Krouse Rosenthal book / written by Candice Ransom ;
pictures based on art by Brigette Barrager.
Description: New York : Random House Children's Books, [2021] |
Series: Step into reading ; step 2 | Audience: Ages 4–6. | Audience: Grades K–1. |
Summary: "When a cold snap hits, Uni must use her special powers to help bring spring back to the land of unicorns, and keep all the animals from freezing." —Provided by publisher.
Identifiers: LCCN 2020008474 (print) | LCCN 2020008475 (ebook) |
ISBN 978-0-593-17806-5 (trade paperback) | ISBN 978-0-593-17807-2 (library binding) |
ISBN 978-0-593-17808-9 (ebook)
Subjects: CYAC: Unicorns—Fiction. | Seasons—Fiction.
Classification: LCC PZ7.R1743 Un 2021 (print) | LCC PZ7.R1743 (ebook) | DDC [E]—dc23

Printed in the United States of America
10 9 8 7 6 5 4 3 2 1

UNI
Brings Spring

Uni the UNICORN

an Amy Krouse Rosenthal book
pictures based on art by Brigette Barrager

Random House 🏠 New York

It has been
a long winter.
Uni cannot wait
for spring.

One day, the sun
shines extra brightly.
The first flowers bloom.
The air feels soft.

5

Uni visits animal friends
in the forest.

Robin is here.

She sings a spring song.

All winter,
Robin lived down south.
Now she gathers grass
for her nest.

Turtle climbs
out of the pond.
All winter,
he lived under the mud.

Now he sits

on a warm rock.

Squirrel jumps
from her tree.
All winter,
she slept in her hole.
Now she looks
for nuts to eat.

Everyone is happy
spring is here!

Then clouds block the sun.
Snowflakes begin to fall.

Soon the ground is
all white.
Icicles hang from
tree branches.
The air is freezing.

Spring has gone!
Winter has come back.

Uni's animal friends
are cold and hungry.
What will they do?

Uni wishes hard.
But a wish
cannot make winter
go away.

Uni will help
in other ways!

Uni spears old leaves
for Robin's nest.

Uni breaks the ice
on the pond.
Turtle slides back
under the mud.

Uni finds nuts

for Squirrel to eat.

Then Uni sees a
new animal.
A bear cub!
The cub is lost!

"Where do you live?"

Uni asks him.

The cub does not know.

"Don't worry," says Uni.

"I will find your home."

They walk through
the woods.

The snow is getting deeper.

The air is getting colder.

Uni sees a cave.

A bear is looking out.

It's the mother bear!

The cub runs toward

his mom.

Then Uni spots
a giant icicle
hanging in the cave.

The icicle could drop.

The bears are in danger!

Uni races to the cave.

Uni can see this is
a magic icicle.
It caused winter
to come back.

Uni's horn can
handle this icicle.
One touch of Uni's horn
makes the icicle glow.

Now rainbows dance
on the cave walls!
Drip! Drip! Drip!

The icicle is melting!
Uni's wish could not
make winter leave.
But unicorn magic worked!

Uni is so happy
to have helped
forest friends.

Soon the snow is gone.

Flowers bloom again.

The air is soft once more.

The animals cheer.

"Spring is here to stay!"
Uni says.
"Let's play!"